ESCAPE TO THE FOREST

ESCAPE TO THE FOREST

Based on a True Story of the Holocaust

Ruth Yaffe Radin
illustrated by Janet Hamlin

■ HarperCollins*Publishers*

The author and publisher would like to thank Nechama Tec, author of *Defiance: The Bielski Partisans*, for her expert help and advice.

Library of Congress Cataloging-in-Publication Data
Radin, Ruth Y.
   Escape to the forest : based on a true story of the Holocaust / by Ruth Yaffe Radin ; illustrated by Janet Hamlin.
      p.   cm.
   Summary: A young Jewish girl living with her family in Lida, Poland, at the beginning of World War II recalls the horrors of life under first the Russians then the Nazis, before fleeing to join Tuvia Bielski, a partisan who tried to save as many Jews as possible. Based on a true story.
   ISBN 0-06-028520-6. — ISBN 0-06-028521-4 (lib. bdg.)
   1. World War, 1939–1945—Jews—Belarus—Lida—Juvenile Fiction. [1. World War, 1939–1945—Jews—Belarus—Lida—Fiction. 2. Holocaust, Jewish (1939–1945)—Belarus—Lida—Fiction.] I. Hamlin, Janet, ill. II. Title.
PZ7.R1216Es   2000   99-26426
[Fic]—dc20   CIP

Typography by Christopher Stengel
1   2   3   4   5   6   7   8   9   10
❖
First Edition

For Sheila, who survived!

—R.Y.R.

For my mom

—J.H.

CHAPTER ONE
Fall 1939

My parents stood at the open front door, facing the darkness, whispering to someone I couldn't see. It was a woman. Her voice sounded serious, maybe frightened, but it was too quiet to understand the words. Everything was supposed to be all right, wasn't it, now that the Russians had come?

Even with her back toward me I could feel my mother protecting me. My father stood next to her, his arm around her shoulders. They didn't know I was listening from the kitchen, looking out through the crack between the frame and the open door. The wind whined and shook the shutters. The wood in the stove crackled, warming the room but making it harder to hear. We were safe in this brick house, weren't we, even though we were Jews?

Then my mother stepped aside. "You may stay here," she said to the stranger, "but you must be hidden."

My father helped with her suitcases. She had on too many clothes for the end of September, and she didn't look any older than my brother, David, who was nineteen.

Why was she staying? Where would she hide? I stepped out from behind the door, walking into the front room.

"Sarah!" my mother said, surprised.

I stared at the stranger, who had started to remove layers of clothing, putting them on my father's easy chair. She smiled awkwardly at me. Neither one of us spoke.

My father reached for my hand. "Sarah is good at keeping secrets," he said, looking at me. "Lili will be staying here in the back room upstairs. Her mother and sisters are gone, and she must have a place to live."

Gone where? What did he mean? And why had she come to our house? My parents didn't say anything about knowing her, or her family.

"Let us see what you brought," my mother said to Lili.

We all watched as she opened the suitcases. They were full of cloth, not clothes. She took out pieces of plain fabric in shades of blue, green and brown, some heavy enough, I guessed, for pants and jackets, some lightweight that I could imagine for dresses and blouses. "I do well selling the cloth," Lili said, showing us money that she had kept in pockets hidden inside her clothing. "I was away from home selling when the Russians—"

My mother cut her off. "The money will help, and we will hide the cloth somewhere else."

Just then my brother came in, closing the door hard against the wind.

"David," I called out happily. I ran to him, expecting that he would lift me high into the air. He started to speak, but when he saw Lili, he stopped. I backed away as they stared at each other.

"This is our son, David," my mother said. "Come, you must be hungry. We will have some soup and talk about what is happening."

A lot was happening. The Russian army had come into eastern Poland almost two weeks ago. There was no fighting that I saw, but our lives were changing here where I lived on the edge of our small town of Lida. The Russians had closed my school because it taught about the Jewish religion, and religion was something they didn't believe in.

Now I went to another school. The Russians had also taken over the foundry where my father hammered and shaped metal into tools. When I asked him why they had done that, he said that the Russians wanted to be in charge of the work people did.

Yet even with the Russians here some things were the same. We still bought food from peasant farmers outside of town. As always, tall, thin Chicava came to pick up our clothes, curtains and bedding to wash before the winter weather. Her skin, lined and old, made her look mean, but she wasn't. She told me stories about enchanted forests and people whose lives were touched by magic. Even now that I was eight, I still listened. My mother said Chicava told fanciful tales and thought they were true. I looked toward the forest and wondered about that. Beyond the fields and the farms was a world I barely knew. We sometimes went into villages at the edge of the forest to buy wood, or to visit Anna and Michal, gentile friends of my parents. But we hadn't followed the paths among the trees into the vast, dark, vine-tangled world that Chicava talked about.

Once Lili settled in with us, I listened to her stories

too. Sometimes I went into the little upstairs room and we sat facing each other on her bed, not strangers anymore as we shared the quilt between us. Her tales seemed just as fanciful as the ones that Chicava told. Only this time my mother didn't say they were untrue. Lili told me about a wicked German leader called Hitler, whose army had taken over western Poland where she used to live. She said that the Germans had forced the Jews all over the countryside to leave their homes, making them go into the cities. But there wasn't room for everyone there.

Maybe that was why every day, as fall leaves crackled under my feet and the ground became harder and colder, more Jews came to Lida, running from the Germans. Just like Lili, they were looking for a safe place to live, hoping someone would take them in. But I still thought that even if terrible things were happening in other places, everything would be all right for us. The Germans weren't here, and in school I was learning Russian.

CHAPTER TWO

Winter 1939–1940

By December I could understand and speak simple Russian sentences. The days were much shorter, and the snow, already deep on the ground, would stay all winter long. I hurried to and from school on paths of packed-down snow that were close to the wooden houses squeezed together in the center of town. One day as I rushed home, feeling my toes grow numb from the cold, I saw Riva up ahead. My family knew hers, and she had two brothers; one of them, Hersh, was David's age. She went to another school and was a year ahead of me. I called to her.

She turned, jumping up and down in place. "I'm freezing."

"I am too," I answered, feeling clumsy as I tried to make my frozen feet move faster, trying to catch up.

"I'm going to keep going," she called. "My mother will worry if I take any longer on such a cold day."

She was right. It was too cold to wait. We'd walk together another time, as we sometimes did.

When I got home, my mother was making latkes, potato pancakes. There was a pot of soup on the stove too. I didn't have to look to know it was barley and potato. Potatoes everywhere—in latkes, in soup, boiled, grated, cut up. Potatoes! In the winter that's what we ate every day. Still, I looked in the pot. Small pieces of meat slowly rose to the surface, then sank out of sight. I breathed in the warmth and the smell of home.

"Tonight is Hanukkah," my mother said, trying to sound cheerful.

"Tonight?" Nobody had said anything till now, and I had forgotten to ask when it would be.

"Papa went to see if he could get candles."

As I hung my coat on a hook, I saw the menorah on the table. My father had made it last year at the foundry, bending and hammering the metal till it became a candle-holder. It would hold eight candles plus one more for the shammas, the candle that would light the others each night.

I sat down on the bench near the stove and took off my shoes. As I rubbed my feet, they began to tingle to life. This Hanukkah would not be like last year's. With the Russians here, I knew, there could be no parties. They had closed the Jewish community center. But we would light candles if Papa could get them. That was the most important thing. And we would sing the blessings.

Just then Lili came into the kitchen. After living with us almost three months, it felt like she was part of the family. "I thought I heard you," she said, and smiled, making me feel warmer already.

"Feel my feet." I held them out, and she grabbed hold of them.

"Ooh! They're cold." And she rubbed them with her fingers. Then with one foot in each hand, she pretended to make them dance, doing a little step with her feet, too, till we both started laughing. Since she had gotten official papers, she didn't have to hide for fear of being sent to

Siberia. I didn't know what papers meant, but my brother had arranged for them, so she was allowed to stay in Lida with our family. David worked as a locksmith and met many people. He did work for them, and in return they helped him. Everyone seemed to need locks now. There were a lot of secrets to keep.

The door opened and my father came in. He reached into his pockets and pulled out some candles.

"It's something. Not enough, but something." There was a heaviness in his voice.

I walked up to him, still barefoot, and felt the chill he had brought in from the cold night. "How many are there?" I asked.

"Ten." He gave them to me. All of Hanukkah fit in one hand. I stared silently at the number of candles that wouldn't be enough. There should have been forty-four. Then I remembered how in the ancient Temple the oil had burned for eight days when it should have lasted for only one. Could we make our own miracle happen?

"Listen," I said, looking from one person to another. "On the first night we light one candle to be the shammas, and use it to light another candle." I put two candles on

the table as I spoke. "On the second night we light two candles with another shammas." I put three more candles down.

"Sarah," my father said. "We know."

"Wait!" I'd speak faster. "On the third night we light three with a shammas." All but one candle was on the table. "We'll have only one candle left for the rest of Hanukkah." I held up the last candle that was in my hand.

My mother shrugged. "We are lucky to have any candles."

"I know. I know. But if we don't use a shammas, and just light one candle each night, there will be enough for the eight days of Hanukkah, with two extra candles. On the last night of Hanukkah we could light three." I looked from one face to another. Lili smiled, but I knew she wouldn't say anything before my parents did. That's what usually happened.

My mother nodded. "It's a good idea."

My father put his arm around my shoulder and gave me a little squeeze. There was no chill left.

When my brother came home, we lit one candle and sat down to eat. My parents faced each other at opposite ends of the table. I sat on one side facing David and Lili on the other. How different they looked from one another— he tall and slender with dark hair, she short and solid-looking with fair hair. Whenever David came into the room, her eyes brightened. Did he like her the way she liked him? At first I didn't think so, but now I couldn't tell.

I tasted the soup my mother always said was seasoned with her love. A plate of latkes waited in the middle of the table. I watched the candle burn. Maybe the Russians didn't want any religion for anyone, but the curtains were closed, and no soldiers had ever come to our door.

CHAPTER THREE

Spring 1940

The winter snows finally melted. At school the sound of Russian was beginning to make me afraid. Soldiers were everywhere now, speaking angrily in this language. The Great Synagogue, tall and grand, with its windows of Jewish Stars high up, was being used by the Russians to store grain. There were more and more rules, and people were being taken away to jail. The Russians sent my uncle Max to frozen Siberia along with many others they thought might be their enemies. My mother said Uncle Max had done nothing wrong, but Aunt Sonia didn't expect to ever see him again.

Aunt Sonia lived a couple of houses away, and I often went there to play with my cousins. Jake and Josef were older than me. Josh was a little younger. The two girls were just past being babies. Sometimes I helped Aunt Sonia with them. My mother told me, "When you go to her house, don't talk about what happened. Aunt Sonia cries too much already." So I never said anything about Uncle Max.

Then one day when I returned home, my mother drew me close and spoke softly. "The Russians arrested Lili. She was out selling some cloth, and they picked her up."

I pulled away. "Why?" I asked. But this time I knew what the answer would be.

"They don't need a reason."

She opened her arms and I rushed back in, wanting to feel safe. "Will they send her to Siberia too?" My body was stiff with fear.

"David is trying now to find out what's happening. Others were arrested also."

It had always been others. But Lili was living with us like a part of our family and they had taken her. David had put locks on our doors, but I didn't think they would keep us safe for long. "Will they come for us?"

My mother didn't answer, but she let go of me. "Come. The rugs need beating. They're full of the dust and the smell of winter. Spring is here."

Why were we doing this now? Why think of cleaning

with Lili in jail? But I helped carry the rugs outside, rag rugs and braided rugs, and hung them over the fence. Then I went back for the heavy wire rug beater. I handed it to my mother and watched as she started on the first rug. She swung at it fiercely, sending dust into the air, her eyes angry, her lips sealed tight. Then she went on to the second one. I pretended each rug was a Russian soldier. That's it. There they were, lined up, waiting.

"Let me do it too," I said.

She wiped her hair off her forehead and silently handed me the beater. While we waited for David, we could beat the Russians lined up on our fence.

It was late when he came home. We sat at the kitchen table and listened.

"I paid off a guard, and he told me that they believe Lili is a German spy." David shook his head in disbelief.

"A German spy? She is a Jew!" My father didn't often raise his voice the way he did now.

"Her blond hair makes her look German," David said.

My mother shook her head. "That's *mishugeh*, crazy!"

My hair was fair too. I touched it and looked at my mother.

"No, no. Don't worry." My mother reached over and stroked my hair. "They do not want children." But she didn't sound certain. None of us could tell what would happen next.

My father put his elbows on the table and rested his head in his hands, the way he always did when he felt really upset.

I hated it when he did that. Was he wishing he had stayed in America, where he had lived for a while? But if he hadn't come back to Lida, he wouldn't have married my mother. He wouldn't have had us.

David stood up and walked around the room. "We have to do something. How can they keep her for such reasons?"

"The Russians fear the Germans," my mother said softly. "When you are afraid, it is easy to be foolish. We will wait and see what happens. Try to get more information, but remember, every bit will cost something. We don't have much."

David started to protest.

"David," my mother said firmly, "what would you do?"

He was silent.

I looked at his pained expression. He liked Lili the way she liked him. Now I knew.

Days passed. A week went by. David made locks. My father worked in the foundry. I went to school. My mother cooked, and Lili was still in jail. David again bribed the guard, who told him that Lili wasn't eating. The next week David went once more, and she still wasn't eating.

At our evening meal he pushed his bowl of soup away. "She'll die," he said quietly, sounding defeated.

My mother reached for his hand. "She is still alive and near us, not on her way to Siberia. Eat," she said gently.

David pushed his chair back quickly, scraping the legs noisily on the floor. He left the room without another word.

I tried to finish eating, but I had trouble swallowing.

Then, on the eighteenth day after Lili's arrest, as I

helped my mother do dishes, there was a loud banging on the front door. My brother opened it. A Russian soldier shoved Lili toward him. "The Jew can die here," he said with hate, and then left.

Weak and hollow eyed, Lili collapsed in David's arms. Was this what dying was? Frightened, I didn't rush to her as my parents did. David lifted her and started upstairs. "You'll be strong again," he said to her. "You're home."

My mother walked hurriedly into the kitchen. "I'll heat some soup."

Lili got stronger, but I worried whenever I thought about what had happened. First the Russians had taken Uncle Max away without any reason. Then they had arrested Lili. I listened more carefully to what was said about the Russians and the Germans. I knew that if they wanted to, they could hurt me, too.

CHAPTER FOUR

Fall 1940–Summer 1941

In September I was back in school, learning Russian history now as well as mathematics. I was nine and no longer with the very young children. My parents talked of how the British Air Force had held off a massive German air attack against England, and I listened.

"Hitler can be defeated," my father said. And my mother agreed.

But this battle far to the west didn't seem real to me.

In December, when the snow was deep on the ground, we celebrated Hanukkah again. But I knew not to talk about such a thing at the Russian school. While the candles burned, I wished that nothing terrible would ever happen to us again in Lida.

But in the middle of June, after school ended for the

year, there were stories that the German army was coming, that planes would drop bombs. My parents told me I would go stay with Aunt Ida and Uncle Sol, who lived in the country about a fifteen-minute walk away.

"You will be safe farther from town," my father said.

I didn't want to go. "How long will I be there?"

"We don't know right now."

"What about you and Mama and David and Lili?"

My mother kissed me. "Don't worry about us. We will be all right."

How could they be all right? But I didn't say that. It wouldn't have made any difference.

The next morning my father and I started off. I looked back once at our sturdy brick house with the locks on the doors, still wishing I didn't have to go. Besides my clothes I took my small white pillowcase. It was embroidered with flowers that I liked to trace with my fingers in the dark before I fell asleep. The sun was shining brightly now as we walked farther into the countryside. At other times I would have run ahead, then waited till my father caught up. But this time I held his hand. Every so often we passed stray chickens pecking at the ground, sticking out their necks, pulling them back in, not minding that we were there too.

As we turned onto a narrow path, walking toward Aunt Ida and Uncle Sol's house, I wondered if the stories about the Germans would come true.

Early Sunday morning we all knew they had. German planes did come. Aunt Ida, Uncle Sol and I ran down into the damp, dark cellar and sat close together on a wooden bench near one of the dirt walls. As we heard explosions in the distance, Uncle Sol mumbled to himself and Aunt Ida kept talking to God. I was afraid without making a sound.

When we were sure the bombing had stopped, we went upstairs and looked out a window. A great cloud of smoke had spread over the only world I knew. I wished it would lift and everything would be the same as before. But I knew it wouldn't be. In the distance we could see that Lida was on fire. The smell of it reached into the countryside. I wanted to run back to my parents and David. I wanted to see Lili, too. What had happened to them?

There was no word the next day, or the next or the next, as we listened to what seemed like endless gunfire. Each time we heard planes overhead, we hid in the cellar.

While the bombs fell in the distance, I closed my eyes so hard they hurt and tried to see everything as it had been.

Finally on Saturday, after the skies had been quiet for almost a day, I saw my brother walking slowly up the path. His left arm was bandaged.

I ran outside. "What happened?"

He drew me close with his good arm. "We're all right, Mama, Papa, Lili and I. But bombs hit our house and Aunt Sonia's."

I shook my head. "We can fix them, can't we?"

"No," David said gently. "We're living with Aunt Sonia and her family in the caretaker's house on her property."

"That's where Chicava lives."

"She's still there. Her husband was killed in the bombing."

I gasped.

"That's not all." David was silent for a moment, then went on. "Cousin Josef was helping me take some things from our house to the caretaker's when some fighter planes flew low." David's voice shook. "We dropped what we were carrying and I held Josef in my arms. But we were out in the open. He was hit in the head and died instantly." Then almost as if he had forgotten, he added, "Some metal tore into my arm."

What he had said about Josef didn't seem real. My cousin was only twelve, not much older than me. I couldn't say anything.

"Sarah, are you all right?" David asked softly.

I nodded, trying not to cry.

When we started walking back to town, we passed some tanks that had been abandoned by the Russian army. The Russians had seemed so powerful until the Germans had come. We passed people leaving town, their arms carrying bundles, their faces full of sadness. German jeeps and trucks roared by, their horns warning us to move out of the way as if we were chickens pecking for food.

At the edge of Lida I saw what was left of our house. There was no second floor. There were no windows, only broken glass. But I stood there forcing myself to look, remembering where everything had been: my father's chair, the kitchen table, the stairway. I felt David's arm around my shoulders.

"I hate Hitler," I whispered, tears finally filling my eyes.

"We all do."

"What will happen now?"

My brother was silent.

"We don't know," I said quietly, "do we?"

He shook his head.

CHAPTER FIVE

Summer 1941

While the fires smoldered, more Germans came in tanks and in trucks. Nobody would go away from the little caretaker's house except for David and Lili. Whenever they returned, my mother would mumble a prayer of thanks. There were eleven of us living in only two rooms, but we didn't complain—not Aunt Sonia, who cried softly when she thought we were all asleep; not Chicava, whose feet had gotten burned during the bombing, so it was hard for her to walk. Josef had died. There were hundreds of others who had died, too, but we had survived.

"Remember that, Sarah," my mother said. "We are lucky."

Before the Germans had come, my parents and my

aunt had been able to save some bedding, pots, dishes and furniture by moving them into the cellars. But there were no rugs to beat now, no curtains to wash. I had the small pillowcase that I had taken into the country with me before the bombing. Sometimes when I stroked it, I could remember what it was like before the Germans, before the Russians.

At night, lying in bed in one room, I would listen to the grown-ups talking quietly in the other room.

"We still have my cloth to trade for what we need," Lili said one night.

We never talked about Lili's cloth, but I knew it was hidden in farmhouses that belonged to gentiles. I remembered going to see Anna and Michal after Lili had come. They had said they would do what they could to help us. But it had to be a secret. My mother told me they could be punished if the Germans found out they were helping Jews. Little by little she was telling me what I'd have to know now that the Germans were here.

Then I heard Chicava. "I can plant vegetables."

"We get them from the farmers," my mother said.

"Maybe not." My father sounded weary.

"The children could help," my aunt said. "It will be something for them to do."

It didn't seem possible that the Germans would go away soon, and I wondered what kind of school I would go to in the fall. Where would it be? My school on Sadowa Street had burned. Would Mr. Rosenberg still be the principal?

The next day we all sat in the bigger of the two rooms listening to my brother. "I found out," David said, "that the Germans are going to appoint Jewish leaders to be on a council, a *Judenrat*, to govern the Jewish community. According to German instructions, of course."

My father was pleased. "It is good that they are appointing Jews."

"How can you be sure?" my brother said bitterly. "We know what has happened west of here. Jews are forced into crowded ghettos. Everything is taken from them." His voice was getting louder. "They are treated like animals. They are dying from disease."

"Stop!" my mother shouted.

I jumped, not used to hearing her speak that way. My littlest cousin, Rivka, began to cry, and my aunt comforted her. Could David be right? I looked at my mother, afraid.

"We don't know how much is true," my mother said more quietly.

David clenched his fists. "Is the bombing of Lida and our house true?"

I looked toward Lili, who had starved herself, wanting to die when she was imprisoned by the Russians. But the Russians hadn't bombed Lida the way the Germans had. The smell of the fires was still in the air. I shuddered. The Russians had been frightening, but the Germans were worse.

"What is better," my mother said, "to argue among ourselves or to do our best under the circumstances?"

Lili spoke. "David and I will try to find out whatever we can."

Maybe David would make locks for the Germans, the way he had for the Russians. And Lili had been arrested because her fair hair made her look like a German. Maybe that would help. I wondered if I looked like a German, with my fair hair. Yet in pictures I had seen, Hitler himself had dark hair like that of Jews I knew in Lida. It was all very confusing.

Then a few days later, as I sat on the front step making

a cradle of string between my fingers, I looked down the road. More men than I could count were walking toward us from the center of town. Jake and Josh were out in back and saw them too. We all ran inside, afraid. My parents and I looked out the window. My aunt and her children went into the other room. Twisting and untwisting the string around my fingers, I watched the group getting closer. They were surrounded by Nazis with guns.

"Where are David and Lili?" My mother's voice shook.

My father patted her shoulder. "It's all right. They told me they were going to a farmhouse to get cloth."

Maybe to Anna and Michal's, I thought.

As the group got closer, the three of us backed away from the window. My mother clasped her hand over her mouth as they began to pass by, heading into the country. I stared out silently. There were Mr. Rosenberg and my older cousin Noah, who lived on the other side of Lida.

"Doctors, rabbis, teachers, the leaders of the community," my father said softly.

"Noah isn't," I whispered. "Why is he with them?"

My father shook his head, puzzled. "Maybe there's work they're needed for." Noah was almost David's age.

I didn't believe that; and I didn't think my parents did either, because we all stayed inside for the rest of the day.

The next day the truth of what had happened spread from family to family. David burst into the house. He pushed against the beds and slammed his hands against the walls, as if trying to make the space larger. My mother started screaming. My father caught hold of him.

"Stop! Stop! What is it? Tell us."

David broke away and stood between the two rooms, leaning against the door frame.

"The two hundred men marched out of town yesterday—dead!"

Nobody spoke.

My mother sank onto a bed. "What happened?" she asked, her voice hoarse.

My teeth began to chatter as if it were the coldest winter day.

"The Germans took them out into the country. They lined everyone up." My brother struggled with the words. "They shot them! Farmers who were forced to do the burying told what happened." His voice trembled, and he began to weep quietly.

I hadn't seen my brother cry since I was very little, and

this scared me almost as much as what he had said. Still I had to ask. "Why was Noah killed?"

He looked at me with clouded eyes. "Others like Noah were caught and condemned because they were in the streets, or nearby." His voice became a whisper. "There is no reason for any of it." Then he fell silent.

My father started rocking back and forth. *"Yisgadal, veyiskadash . . ."* He was saying Kaddish.

The ancient prayer seemed to bring us closer together. Even though I couldn't understand the words, I knew they were supposed to remind us that there was still God.

David and Lili kept bringing back news. We knew that some Russian soldiers had escaped to the forest to save themselves, and now there was talk of them organizing into partisan units to fight the Germans.

"The farmers are afraid of them," David said. "They show up at farmhouses demanding food and arms."

"Maybe they'll help the Jews," Aunt Sonia said.

Lili's eyes filled with hate. "Russians wouldn't help Jews."

David put his hand gently on her shoulder. "By fighting the Germans, they would be helping us."

In the meantime we heard of more and more Jews who were heading east, trying to outrun the Germans. "Could we go too?" I asked my mother once, as she kissed me good night.

She stroked my hair. Hers, fair like mine, was untied now and fell over her shoulders. She didn't answer.

We stayed. I helped Chicava in the garden. Her burns had healed into ugly scars, but she didn't complain. I tried not to stare at her feet. There was no talk of school in the fall. David got working papers from the Germans, so he was making locks for them now.

"We'll be safe if I am useful to them," he told me one night as we looked at the summer sky from the front step. He put his arm around my shoulder and squeezed me close.

"Are you afraid when you're with them?"

He shrugged his shoulders. "I do what they tell me to do, and I don't say much unless they ask me a question.

Most of the time they don't even look at me."

"Do you look at them?"

"If I have to."

"I think you are brave," I said. He seemed so grown up. I decided then it was time for me to be grown up too. I was already ten.

CHAPTER SIX

Fall 1941

I n October, after ordering Christians away from their homes in the outskirts of Lida, the Germans commanded all the Jews to get ready to move into these empty houses. We sat in the larger of our two rooms to talk about this new development.

My father spoke first. "We must do as they say without questions. We don't want to be thought of as troublemakers."

"We are not the ones at fault," David said tightly, trying to keep his anger in check.

Lili took his hand but looked at my parents. "In the Warsaw ghetto Jews die from the crowding, disease, not getting enough food. We have all heard about that."

My mother shook her head. "But Lida is much smaller.

Do you see any starving? We'll still get food from the peasants. This isn't Warsaw. It's different."

"What street will we live on?" I asked.

Nobody knew.

When the day came, we filled a wagon my father had borrowed with blankets and quilts, a small table, pots and pans, cups, bowls and our clothes. My brother and father would pull it. The rest of us carried sacks and baskets with whatever else we had—the menorah, a few family pictures, a piece of a mirror. There was so little, compared to what we had had before the bombing. My mother brought barley and potatoes for soup, just in case it would be hard to get food. I put my pillowcase in one of my pockets.

Chicava stood silently at the door as we were ready to start off. She could stay in the house that belonged to my family, but we couldn't, just because she was Christian and we were Jewish. Yet other Christians had been chased away from their homes to make room for us. I didn't think I'd ever understand the Germans. Chicava didn't say anything, but I saw her wipe a tear from her eye. I nodded to her, shifting my sack on my shoulder, my thoughts shifting as well to what might happen next.

As we walked into town along Suwalska Street, we saw other families we knew, many struggling to carry their belongings without wagons. I saw Riva, and other friends from my school, but nobody called out to anybody. Jews would be coming from other towns, too, David had said. They were places I knew nothing about, except for their names—Traby, Duoly and Lipniškzi. What would the Germans do with all the houses that had been left in those places?

We were assigned to a building on Zawalna Street with floors that creaked loudly beneath our feet. Other families would live there also, and were beginning to arrive. We found an empty room and unloaded our things. While David and Lili went to return the wagon, the rest of us stood in what was to be our new home. Was this a ghetto like the one in Warsaw? I tried to guess who had lived here before. There were beds, but not enough for everyone.

"One room for all of us," my father said heavily. We heard other families talking and moving about in the other rooms.

Aunt Sonia sighed. "How are we to manage?" My cousins were already opening the sacks. "Wait, wait," she

scolded. "We don't know where we'll put things yet."
There was one cabinet and some shelves.

"We're lucky the room has a stove," my mother said.
"We'll be able to cook, and in the winter . . ." She didn't
finish what she started to say. We kept being lucky, I
thought sadly, having less and less.

I tried to picture what it would be like living here.
Right now we could barely move, with everything piled at
our feet. I stepped over some sacks to a bed. "It smells," I
complained. "I don't even want to sit on it." My parents
didn't answer, and I was sorry that I had said anything.

All of a sudden we heard shots.

I started toward the window to look out.

"No!" My mother grabbed my arm, and I stopped.
Then she spoke more calmly. "This isn't like before."

I nodded, putting my hands in my pocket, feeling my
pillowcase.

We settled into this new place that even my mother
called a ghetto. There was no school. Instead, I collected
scraps of wood from broken fences and from the ruins of
buildings burned in the bombing. We used them in our
stove to heat the water we pumped from the outside well.

The Germans made everyone who could be useful to them work without pay. David still made locks and did other mechanic's jobs. Lili was assigned to a crew that shoveled coal all day long to heat the barracks where the Germans lived. She returned each night, black with coal dust and sore from her forced labor. Both she and David had to wear yellow Stars of David on their clothes to show they were Jewish. My father was not assigned work because of his age. He was already in his sixties. He mostly helped my mother in the daily routines.

We were still able to go out of town during the day. We went to farmers we knew, secretly trading Lili's cloth for eggs, beets and potatoes. Sometimes we went to see Chicava. "Here," she would say, shoving a small sack of potatoes into my hands. The Nazis had made it against the law to sell or give food to Jews. Careful to hide what we had, we were never stopped and asked to explain where we were going or what we were doing.

Those in the ghetto who came from places other than

Lida had a harder time. They didn't know anyone nearby and had to survive on the small food ration the Nazis gave them. Farmers who used to gather in the marketplace off Suwalska Street and sell what they grew were not allowed to do that anymore. It was too close to where the Jews lived. The Nazis meant to starve us.

Even though my family was better off than many, my father and my mother looked thinner to me than they had before we moved to Zawalna Street. They said it was my imagination. I would argue when they gave me their bread or their potato, but I ate it just the same.

When I went out into the streets of the ghetto to see my friends from school, we would hear shots sometimes. We'd run inside the closest building. There were Jewish policemen assigned by the Nazis to keep order, but they had no guns. They weren't the ones shooting. We were getting used to seeing wagons carrying the dead to the stone-walled cemetery outside the ghetto. But somehow nobody shot us.

Then one day when I was helping my mother shake the bedding out the window, a soldier out in the street looked over and called to her.

"Come here," he yelled. He and another German soldier

were talking to a young woman who was holding a baby.

My mother pulled back inside, yanking the bedding with her.

I grabbed hold of her. "No! No!"

"It's all right," she whispered, holding me against her. "You will be fine. You are almost grown up." She looked around frantically. We were alone. Lili and David were working. My aunt was out with the children, looking for fresh air and sunshine. Where was my father? Playing cards? Even in this place it was possible to find five minutes of pleasure.

"Stay here," my mother commanded. "Wait for Papa." Then she left without turning back. I watched, trying to stay hidden near the edge of the window. The woman who held the baby was pleading with the soldiers. I could tell that, but I couldn't hear what she said. One of the soldiers snatched the baby from her and handed it to my mother, ordering her away. The young woman started to follow my mother. The German raised his gun. He fired. The young woman staggered. "My baby," she cried.

There was another shot, and her body fell and lay still. I watched my mother walk stiffly toward our building, holding the baby, not turning around. Would they shoot her, too? The Germans began to laugh, then walked away. I couldn't move, my breath coming in short gasps.

When my mother came in, her eyes were staring straight ahead. I ran to her, screaming.

"No!" She covered my mouth with her hand. The baby began to cry, shaking its head from side to side. My mother became alive again and began cooing to comfort this tiny stranger.

The baby was a girl. My parents guessed she was about five months old, and she was ours now. We called her Rachel. With a baby there were needs we hadn't had before. Milk was rationed, and we were able to get only what the Germans would allow. It was never enough.

We needed cloth for diapers, and my mother ripped strips from our bedding to make them. "You will have to do with a little less," she told us.

She didn't have to say that. It was what we had been doing for a long time.

We had to wash diapers, even if we didn't wash our clothes very often. Sometimes we got soap that the peasants made, but we used ashes more often. There were enough of those.

The weather turned bitter and the snow fell. Our wooden building creaked, and there were drafts that came in around the windows. But we were careful not to burn precious wood in our stove unless we needed it for heating water or for making soup. We would get some warmth from the heat meant for something else. Every night, hungry and cold, Rachel would wake and cry. My mother rocked her in her arms and sang, "*Un-ter Yi-de-les vi-ge-le*, There's a wee little goat so snowy white, Who will come to your cradle in the night, With roses, raisins and almonds. . . ." Sometimes the lullaby would help Rachel fall asleep, but there would never be roses, raisins and almonds for her.

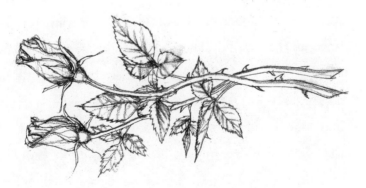

CHAPTER SEVEN

Spring 1942

In March there was still snow on the ground, but it wasn't white. There were too many feet trampling it. There were trails of ashes, and splatters of blood where the Nazis had killed Jews.

"Show me your working papers," they'd shout to someone they'd stopped on the street. But it might not matter if that person had papers or not. If the Nazis wanted to kill someone, they would. They kept issuing new papers, but never as many as before. That way they could kill, kill, kill and say there was a reason. When would the cemetery be filled up? Soon, I thought. Even some of the living looked dead as they lay sleeping against the walls of our building. I was always cold. The winter seemed years long, and the people around me looked older than they should have.

Their steps were slow, their backs bent, and their eyes watery with tears that never went away. Our family was still getting food from the outside, but not as much as before. And we had to make sure to hide it, or it might be stolen.

David and Lili came back to the ghetto each night, tired from their work, and told us what they had heard beyond the crowded room with the stove, beyond the wooden building with the creaking floors, beyond our corner of Lida where everyone waited for something to happen. We huddled together on the beds, trying to stay warm, listening.

"Even some Jews are living in the forest, now," David said. "One family called Bielski goes to farms with guns and demands food to survive, just like the Russian soldiers who escaped."

Would we be able to do what the Bielskis did? I could picture my brother with a gun, but not anybody else in the family.

Then one night my brother whispered, "There are camps. Someone who escaped from one said the Nazis tell Jews that they will be sent there to work. But it isn't so.

First they are packed into trains like animals. There is barely enough air to breathe. Then there is a 'selection' when they arrive at the camps. Those sent to the left live. Those sent to the right die."

"No!" My father kept shaking his head.

"It is true," Lili said.

"Monsters!" My mother began stroking Rachel's hair.

I thought of Rachel's mother. "Who lives and who dies?" I asked, wanting and not wanting to know at the same time.

My brother and Lili looked at each other. "They save those who are strong and able to work," David said.

"Like you and Lili."

"Maybe."

I looked at my parents, Aunt Sonia and my cousins. Would they live? Would I? I was afraid to ask the question out loud. The Nazis had let Rachel live, and she was only a baby.

When warm weather finally came, we opened the windows, trading the smells of people crowded together inside for the shouts of soldiers outside. I also saw Chicava again. I hadn't seen her all winter. She let me help her plant the garden. We put in onions, potatoes and beets.

"Chicava," I said when my mother wasn't nearby, "there are camps." And I told her what David had told us.

She didn't look at me. "Your family will take care of you," she said. Then she made a cross sign on herself. I didn't understand what that meant exactly, though I had seen other Christians do it, too. I knew she was upset by what I had said. None of the stories she had told me had ever frightened me as much as what I knew now about the Nazis.

Then one morning in May, before we were ready to wake up, we heard a commotion outside. There were shots, screams. Careful not to show himself, David looked out a corner of the window. "There are SS everywhere."

I bit my lip. We all feared these savage Nazi police units.

"They're going into the buildings." David backed into the room.

"It is our time," my father said softly, rocking back and forth on the edge of the bed.

"Stop," my mother said. "Our tradition says, 'As long as a man breathes, he should not lose hope.' It is not the end yet. Quickly, everyone, put on your shoes and as many clothes as you can."

We all did as she ordered. My shoes still fit from last year; my jacket, too. Eleven sounded grown up, but I thought I still looked ten. How many potatoes, I wondered, fumbling with my jacket buttons, would I have to eat to make me look eleven? But then my clothes wouldn't fit. I put my comb in one pocket, my crumpled pillowcase in another. Maybe I was lucky to still be small.

My aunt began to cry.

My mother reached up, shaking her arms as if arguing with God. "We are family," she said. "We must stay together." Rachel began tugging at her leg and my mother picked her up, then grabbed a blanket to wrap her in.

David put his arm around Lili. "We will be married someday."

There was silence, as if his words, so full of hope, needed time to reach us as we heard the angry shouts of the Nazis outside. But they were not yet in our building.

My father stood up and put one hand on my brother's shoulder and one on Lili's. "You have my blessing." He kissed each of them. "May God bless you both.

May God bless us all."

It seemed almost like a wedding as we each kissed Lili and David solemnly.

Then I went toward the window. I knew not to stand right in front of it. SS, armed with guns and iron bars, were shouting to those already outside to line up by family. Some of the Jews hadn't had time to put shoes on and were stepping barefoot on the cobblestones. One of the Nazis aimed his gun into the air and fired, but no Jews were hit that time. I stepped back, tripping over a pile of bedding.

My brother caught me and gave me a hug. I hugged him back, not wanting to let go. "We will get through this," he whispered as we heard the SS stomp into our building.

"Everyone out!" they yelled, banging on the doors. But there was no need for words. Their boots spoke, commanding us to obey.

My father looked at each one of us. "We will go in dignity." Then he opened the door to the hallway. An officer pushed past us into the room. He bent over to see if anyone might be hiding under the beds. Then he shoved us ahead of him into the hall before banging on other doors. My mother stumbled, and my father caught hold of her. Rachel started crying in her arms.

"Shhhh! Shhhhh!" I said, trying to make her smile, worrying that she would attract too much attention to us once we were outside. As we walked into the street, the day was just beginning, yet it seemed dark.

"Move, Jewish scum," an officer shouted.

I wouldn't look at him. I wasn't scum. My family wasn't scum, but we walked as he ordered, seeing others come out of their buildings. Soon the streets were filled with all the Jews of Lida. Murderous Nazis were on each side of us with their guns ready, shouting us on past the marketplace into Suwalska Street. They swung their iron bars, hitting whomever they singled out, kicking, then shooting old people. Rabbi Rabinowitz stumbled near us, blood running down his beard, his lips moving in prayer. I felt faint.

Lili grabbed hold of me. "You're all right, Sarah. You're all right."

"Maybe there is a way out," my brother whispered as we were herded toward the railroad tracks that crossed the street at the end of town. "I've done work for some of them. I have papers."

My father turned to my mother. "He still has dreams."

"Look ahead," my brother said, alarmed. "Just this side of the tracks, the Nazis are separating the people into two groups. It's a selection."

My mother put her hand to her mouth, muffling a cry. There is no way out, I thought.

When we got to the officers, they didn't care about our papers and we were ordered to the right with the bigger group, the one with Rabbi Rabinowitz. "They will kill us if we stay here. They would never let a rabbi live," my brother said, looking around frantically. Guards surrounded us all. "Over there! I recognize one of them. I made locks for him." David pushed through the crowd toward the Nazi. "Come."

We followed him. If anyone could save us, it would be David.

"Officer," my brother said, trying to get the guard's attention.

The man turned, hate in his eyes. Then his expression softened a bit as he recognized David.

"Remember I made locks for you? See my papers!" He thrust them at the Nazi. "I am valuable to the German army. And this is my family. Can you help us?"

"Who is here?" The guard spoke quietly, hardly moving his mouth.

"My parents, my sisters, my wife-to-be, my aunt and her children."

He looked at us. Jake and Josh were carrying their little sisters. "The aunt and her children stay here. The rest of you go quickly to the other group."

"Please," Aunt Sonia begged, grabbing hold of his arm.

"Do not touch an officer, Jew." And he pushed her to the ground. I stepped back as if he had struck me. Aunt Sonia lay limp, almost as if she had fainted. My mother, still holding Rachel, tried to help her up, but my father quickly pulled my mother away from her.

"There is nothing we can do," he said gently.

I felt someone tugging at my arm. "Come," Lili whispered. "We have the chance to live."

She didn't let go of my arm and pulled me till my legs started working again. "We're family," I said weakly as we ran to the other group. "My mother says we have to stay together."

"If you stayed there, then the whole family would die. Some will survive this way. You will survive, Sarah."

Then I felt my father, my mother and my brother close to us. My mother was weeping quietly, absently stroking Rachel's back. "We have left Sonia to die. Why should we live and not her, not her children?"

David spoke firmly. "It is not our fault. We did not condemn them."

"Whoever can live must," my father said. "That is the only way to defy the Nazis."

CHAPTER EIGHT

Spring–Summer 1942

Soon after the selection we were ordered back to the ghetto, hearing guns firing in the distance. Those people who had been forced to cross the railroad tracks were lost now. We had seen them being driven on toward the army barracks at the edge of the woods. Others around me cried, but I couldn't. What was wrong with me? All I could think of was that I was alive, and I was glad. My parents, David, Lili and little Rachel were alive, and I was glad. Again we were lucky, but for how much longer?

"If only we had guns," my brother whispered angrily as we walked along. "We should have gone into the forest before the winter."

"The forest in the winter?" My mother shook her head wearily. "It was hard enough to survive the cold in Lida."

"The Bielskis have survived," he said.

We were led to streets where barbed wire was being unrolled and fastened to poles and buildings to make a fence. We would be enclosed on all sides, living in Lida but separate from most of it. The Nazis meant our world to be even smaller now—five streets, six, seven? "How many?" I asked Lili, who was walking next to me. "How big do you think this ghetto is?"

She shrugged her shoulders. "It is nothing by nothing. And there can't be many more than a thousand of us left to live here."

We were assigned to a building on Czerwona Street. We would share one room with two other families this time. The twelve of us stood awkwardly in the space smaller than the room we had lived in before. The Dubnows had a boy and a girl younger than me, and the Mendels were alone. The walls hardly muffled the sounds of survivors in other rooms, mourning those they had lost. I wanted to believe that Aunt Sonia and my cousins were still alive, but I knew that couldn't be true. My face twisted in pain as I looked at what had been left behind by those who had lived here before us. There were crumpled blankets, a few dishes, a pot, a basket—not very different from what we had left behind.

"We'll stay at this end," my mother finally said to the other families, "if that is all right. There are two beds, so . . ."

Mrs. Dubnow began to cry. Her husband tried to comfort her. "We must do the best we can," he told her. Then he whispered something we couldn't hear.

By the next day we were completely closed in by barbed wire.

"Just like the ghettos to the west, just like the camps where Jews are being sent to die," Lili said angrily.

Then she and David told us what they had found out about the Jews who had crossed the railroad tracks.

Lili spoke softly. "There were trenches already dug. Some fell into them, pretending to have been shot. They were hidden by the dead bodies that fell on top of them. Others scrambled away into the woods when the soldiers turned their backs."

"About two hundred escaped, two hundred out of more than five thousand," my brother said, his head bowed. Nobody spoke. Nobody needed to say that my aunt and cousins hadn't survived. "Some survivors are heading east to join the Russian army," he went on. "Others are going to the forest. That's where we should go," he said, looking up at my mother.

She wasn't convinced. "The baby won't survive there. Neither will Sarah, nor Papa, nor I. But if you and Lili want to go, then go." She shrugged her shoulders. "Every war ends. We have a better chance of living if we stay here." She looked around. "Even here."

I didn't know which one to believe.

Lili and David didn't want to leave us, so they didn't go into the forest. David still worked as a locksmith and mechanic. Lili no longer shoveled coal, for of her work crew only she and one other young woman had survived. They were assigned to peel potatoes for the Germans in their barracks, and Lili was able to bring some peels and scraps back for us. At the same time David and Lili brought back scraps of stories.

We sat at our end of the room and listened as David told us that now Tuvia Bielski and his younger brothers, Asael and Zus, were taking Jews other than their relatives into their group in the forest. "They are forming an *otriad*, a partisan detachment," he said. "If they can get arms to fight the Germans, so much the better."

"How is anyone to get arms?" my father said. "The Germans shoot anyone who owns a gun."

"Even so," Lili said, "some have been hidden. They are like gold. There are a few here, a few there. Some are hidden in the countryside, some are even here in the ghetto, smuggled in. They are left over from the Russian army. Some of the peasants might sell them to the partisans."

Did Lili know where there were weapons? She and David didn't tell us how they knew what they knew, but I believed what they said. Still, I wanted to know more. "If we wanted to join the Bielskis, how would we find them?"

My mother sighed. "Sarah, Sarah."

But David's eyes lit up. "Guides from the otriad sneak into the ghetto and lead people out, taking them to a house where they will be hidden. Then someone else takes them from there into the forest to the otriad."

It sounded fantastic. "Where in the forest?" I asked.

"Nobody knows. We think they move from place to place so they won't be found."

The stories continued during the next months. When young people disappeared from the ghetto, we all believed they were going to Bielski's otriad. But we stayed. We could still cook, sharing a wood-burning stove with many families in our building, and we were lucky that Lili was working where she was, getting the food scraps she did. But it was getting harder to smuggle much else to eat into the ghetto, even for those of us who knew people on the outside. Each time gentiles supplied us with food, they were risking their own lives. Still, we had more than others. Those who had only food rations never had enough of the watery soup from the central kitchen to keep them from fainting with hunger.

We weren't allowed to leave this ghetto. But there were gaps in the barbed wire that the Nazis must not have known about, and I begged my parents to let me sneak through the openings to visit Chicava by myself.

"We live closer to the little house now," I argued. "And I'm eleven. I can bring back food, too. The Nazis don't pay as much attention to children as they do to grown-ups. When they see my fair hair, they won't think I'm Jewish."

"There is great danger," my mother said softly, "even for children." But she finally let me go. "Be careful, little one. You are worth far more than a few potatoes."

Sometimes I'd meet Riva at one of the gaps. Her family

was assigned to live just outside the ghetto, at the brewery where they worked at forced labor. As she was sneaking into the ghetto to see her friends, I was sneaking out. We wouldn't talk, but we'd nod, sharing our secret, grasping each other's hand for a moment as we defied the Nazis.

Yet at night, back in the ghetto, back in our room that smelled of too many people, that crawled with lice, I lay on the floor near my parents, near David and Lili, near little Rachel, and I felt safer with them than outside with Chicava. Not because she would have turned me in, but because this was my family. I heard the breathing of the others in our room. I could tell one from another in the dark now. Mr. Dubnow snored loudly. Mrs. Mendel sighed even in her sleep. Perhaps she was dreaming of her son, who had disappeared to the east. Abe and Minna, the Dubnows' chil-

dren, had nightmares, but everyone understood. We were still alive, and nobody complained. I fingered my pillowcase stuffed with my sweater and jacket, thinking of those sweet visits on the outside, walking along the road with my blond hair blowing. Perhaps I would turn twelve before I died.

CHAPTER NINE
Fall 1942–Summer 1943

The summer had passed, and Jews laboring in the fields helped bring in the harvest. Wheat filled the granaries in the country, but there was no hope of its feeding us. It was for the German army. Still in the ghetto, we waited for a starving winter. While some had escaped to the forest, David and Lili had not, choosing to stay with us. I looked at the autumn sky, at the stars, and wondered if there was a world up there I couldn't see, where there was no war.

Then one night, as we tried to sleep, we heard what sounded like many planes droning overhead.

"Will we be bombed?" My voice shook as I reached for my mother's hand. We all huddled together in the darkness, listening to the planes and the stirrings from the other rooms. I tried not to think that this might be the end as I kept my eyes squeezed shut, remembering our brick house, the road out into the country through the fields, the straw roofs of the farmhouses, the good smell of books when I used to go to school. Then the planes began to sound more distant. No bombs had been dropped. I opened my eyes. We were all right.

My father looked out our small window. "I don't see even one Nazi."

For now we were safe.

The next night, when David and Lili came back to the ghetto after their day's labor, they told us what had happened.

"Bielski's partisans set the granaries on fire," David said. "The Germans are worried. As I worked, I heard them talking among themselves."

Lili nodded. "At the barracks, too, I heard them say that Russian airplanes dropped bombs on the granaries to help the Bielskis. Those must have been the planes we heard last night. The Germans think Tuvia Bielski and the Russians planned it together."

My mother shook her head. "I didn't think I would be thankful for the Russians."

"Tell us more about Tuvia Bielski," I said, thinking he was the bravest person alive.

David smiled at me. "That's all we know right now."

Soon after the attack the Germans promised a reward for the capture of the Bielski brothers, or for information leading to their arrest. Nobody turned them in. A short time later we heard that the Bielskis had ambushed German supply trucks. Perhaps the Germans could be defeated after all.

I think that hope helped us survive the winter. Nobody in our room died. Nobody in our room caught typhus in spite of all the lice. They left tiny yellow spots on the snow as they dropped frozen from our clothes while we stood in lines at the filthy outhouse or as we waited to get what little food was rationed to us. Luckily, we still got food from the outside, so we were not starving, too weak to walk as others were. There were no tears, either. We struggled to stay alive, dry-eyed and stubborn.

With spring we opened the windows wide and felt the breeze of a new season. We had been here almost a year. I looked at myself in the small piece of mirror we had rescued so long ago from our house. I was twelve, and yes, I was alive. But just as I'd thought I didn't look eleven last year, I didn't think I looked twelve now.

Yet I wasn't a little girl anymore. My eyes told me that.

By summer news spread that the Nazis were liquidating the ghettos everywhere, sending the Jews in them to the camps to be put to death. Even from Warsaw, where those in the ghetto fought back bravely, there was no more word after the middle of May.

"If we went into the forest, we could save ourselves," David kept telling us. "The Russian partisans are organized now so they can fight the Germans more effectively. They've won control over whole sections of the forest, and Tuvia Bielski works with them while he protects the Jews who live in his otriad. We hear from his guides. They sneak into Lida more and more at night to lead people out."

"They could lead us out too," I said, believing Bielski could make anything happen.

David agreed. "They don't tell us everything, but we think there are hundreds, people of all ages, already in the otriad somewhere in the Nalibocka Forest."

"If you think it will save you, then go into the forest," my father said to him quietly. "But we can't go."

"Why not?" I argued. "David is right. We all should go."

My parents were silent. Then my mother spoke gently yet firmly. "You are just a little girl, so delicate. The forest would be more cruel than this ghetto."

Delicate? I looked down at my worn shoes, my skirt, ragged at the edges and dull from scrubbing that didn't get it clean. I felt my matted hair.

"I'll comb it," Lili said, trying to cheer me, a tired smile on her face after her day's labor. She held out her rough, callused hand, and I reached into my pocket for my comb.

"It's not quite dark. We'll go outside and do it." She didn't have to say that the lice would fall to the ground that way.

As I felt my hair begin to loosen, I wanted to believe that I could be beautiful. "Do you think the war will end before we die?" I asked Lili.

"Look up," Lili said. I tilted my head back. A few stars were shining already, even here. Then I felt the comb pulled hard through my hair.

I was surprised. "What?" I asked. Lili was always gentle.

"We must live, Sarah," she whispered. "We *must*!"

CHAPTER TEN

Fall 1943

David and Lili stayed with us, but we all knew that Lida's future was grim. The day we had feared finally came the third week in September. The Nazis began liquidating our ghetto. As before, we were ordered out of our building by the SS and forced to walk down the middle of Suwalska Street toward the railroad tracks. I could hear David and Lili whispering as they followed close behind us, but I didn't pay attention. I thought only of where we were going, knowing that what would happen to us now would be more horrible than living behind barbed wire, more horrible than living in the wild forest.

Nazis fired their guns. We kept walking. There were screams. We kept walking. Soon we were out of the ghetto, walking between gentiles from Lida, who stood on both sides of the road, doing nothing to help us. Could they even do anything now? My parents were silent. There was nothing to say as we continued along Suwalska Street. When I saw the boxcars in the distance waiting to take us to a dreaded camp, I wanted to turn back, but I knew I had to keep going. Would I be allowed to live? What would happen to my parents? I turned around, searching, then tugged at my mother's arm.

"Where are David and Lili?"

She turned her head quickly, one way, then the other, and looked at me with tears in her eyes. "Perhaps they are trying to save themselves, going to Bielski's. Till now I thought you would be safer with us."

I shivered. September wasn't supposed to be this cold. I wrapped my scarf around my hair and felt my folded pillowcase in my pocket. Rachel whimpered in my mother's arms. My father walked close to me on the other side. I looked away from the Nazis with their guns on either side of us. I wanted to pretend this wasn't real. But I knew it was. Inside I cried for being twelve, and knowing I probably would not be thirteen.

"Sarah!"

I turned and saw Riva frantically making her way toward us.

"I got caught here in the ghetto when they ordered the evacuation," she said, next to me now. It wouldn't matter to the Nazis that she lived at the brewery. She took hold of my arm. "I must get away. My family has plans to meet someplace if we are separated. I think my brothers are still with my parents. I'm the only one who's not."

"Take Sarah with you," my mother commanded in a voice barely a whisper. Then she looked at me with dry eyes, with love that I would always remember. "You have a chance to escape. We are old, your father and I. Think only of saving yourself. Watch for your chance before we get to the trains. Don't look back." Then she looked straight ahead.

My father nodded, gently pushing me from between them, then taking my mother's arm. "Go," he whispered to me. "You must live."

I watched them walk ahead as if I weren't there. I wanted to yell, Mama! Papa, don't leave me! Then Riva pulled me to the edge of the procession and I couldn't see them anymore. Sobs tried to come out, but I willed them to stay in as we walked among Jews closer to the sidewalk.

"Faster!" a soldier ahead of us shouted, shoving an old man who was lagging behind.

This was our chance. "Think only of saving yourself! You must live!" Those were my parents' words. I reached up, pulling the scarf from my head, letting my blond hair show, as I had before when I was outside the ghetto. The Nazis might mistake me for a gentile and not stop us.

Riva and I edged into the crowd who watched the march to the boxcars as if it were a parade. Nobody paid any attention to us, and we kept walking. There were shots, and I shuddered. But none of the bullets hit us. We kept going till fewer and fewer people were around us. Then finally, at the edge of town, fields opened up on both sides of the road, ones I had seen before. I had walked this way a long time ago with my mother and father when we went to visit Anna and Michal.

My throat tightened. "I shouldn't have left my parents," I said.

"You had to." Riva sounded annoyed. "We'll meet my family, then go into the forest." She walked a little faster.

"Hurry up!" Did she really want me with her? Silently I wondered if David and Lili were still alive. Why had they disappeared without a word? Could they really be going to Bielski's otriad?

A wagon rolled by us as we kept to the side of the road. It was driven by a peasant, and a girl about our age sat on its bed of hay. Her feet were bare, and she looked at us suspiciously.

After they had passed, Riva said, "She wanted our shoes."

"We don't look like we belong here."

"We don't belong here," Riva said bitterly. "But we don't belong in a boxcar either."

A late-afternoon wind blew across the fields, bending the wild grasses, and I felt the cold through my thin jacket. I looked toward the sky, but the sun was nowhere. There was only grayness. I was hungry. I had eaten a piece of stale bread this morning. My parents hadn't eaten even that much.

Just then we heard some dogs barking. Where were they? We gasped, seeing them on the road way up ahead with soldiers following close behind.

"Germans!" Riva whispered.

We ran into the fields. Thorny bushes tore at our clothes and skin as we pushed deeper into the wildness that might hide us.

The dogs kept barking, sounding closer and closer.

"Hurry," Riva snapped, pushing some tall weeds apart. Then she disappeared from my sight behind some bushes.

My heart pounded. Had the peasants in the wagon told the Germans about us? My feet got caught in a tangle of thorny vines, and my shoes came off. I kept going. Where was Riva? I heard branches crack. Was that her, or were the Germans getting closer? I bent over, keeping my head down, running till I could no longer catch my breath. Then I crawled beneath the drooping branches of a bush. Shaking, half from cold and half from terror, I waited.

Finally the dogs sounded more distant and there was no more shouting. But I stayed where I was till the sky darkened, listening to sounds without names, seeing shapes that were shadowy except for their eyes. Was Riva hiding too, or had they caught her? I wanted to believe she was all right. At last I crawled out from under the branches and slowly stood up.

"Riva?" I whispered. "Riva?"

I looked around, but there was nobody. She was gone. I sank down onto the cold ground. "Riva! Riva! They found you," I whispered, rocking back and forth. I thought of my parents and Rachel, alive, dead. Which? I thought of my brother. You can't be dead, David. I'll find you. I'll find you and Lili. I swear I will.

I looked for my shoes, not sure of the way I'd run. I'd never find them in the dark, but I couldn't wait till dawn. Someone might see me. I made my way closer to the road to get a better sense of direction. But I didn't dare walk on it out in the open. I'd head toward Anna and Michal's village. They'd help me. Then I'd find Bielski's otriad in the forest. David, I prayed, please be there. My bare feet felt every stone and twig. The cold earth made my toes numb.

At last I saw lights. But as I got closer to the village, I heard drunken laughter and German being spoken. I stopped. There were Nazi soldiers in a house to the left. I knew Anna and Michal lived farther up on the other side of the road. I could trust them, couldn't I? But others here might be sympathizers who would turn me in. I walked in the shadows. A lamp was on in Anna and

Michal's house, and I went to the back door, listening. There were no strangers inside. I knocked lightly.

"Who is it?" Michal's voice was quiet.

I didn't speak. Someone else might hear. I knocked again.

Michal looked out the window and stared, shocked, when he caught sight of me. I looked down at my torn clothes and bare feet. His face showed me what I really looked like. I touched my tangled hair, embarrassed.

The lamp went out and the door opened a crack. "Where are your parents?"

I told him, and he was silent. "If the Nazis find out you're here, they'll burn our house and kill us," he said.

I looked at him, tears filling my eyes for the first time since I had escaped. Anna stood behind him wringing her hands, looking away from me.

"I'm hungry," I whispered, "and my feet . . ." I couldn't speak as I looked down at them, bloody and cold.

"Wait," Michal whispered, and he closed the door. The wind gusted, and I stood with my back against the house, watching. After a few minutes, Michal opened the door again, shoving a bundle into my arms.

"Here, some food, and some clogs for your feet. But you can't stay." His voice was tense. "And you must never tell anyone where you got these things. Tonight you can sleep in the barn. There is a horse blanket and some hay. Before dawn I will wake you and show you a path, only for feet, that leads to the next village. You will be safer there, for it is in partisan hands. Someone there will tell you how to reach Bielski's otriad. That is your only chance." He stopped talking and wiped his eyes awkwardly with his arm.

"Thank you," I whispered, my voice almost disappearing.

Michal nodded, then turned and went inside. They didn't light the lamp again. I didn't think they would turn me in, not after giving me food and shoes. But I wasn't sure. As I went into the barn, their horse whinnied, shaking its head. I stood still.

"Don't give me away," I whispered.

It let out a snort and then was quiet. I slipped into the clogs. The hard wooden soles felt strange. The blanket was on a peg, and I quickly wrapped up in it, accepting its filthiness and roughness with its warmth. Then, sitting on a stool, I began eating the bread and potatoes Michal had given me. I wanted to make them last, but needing them right now, I ate quickly. After I finished, I stuffed a little straw into my pillowcase. Then I lay down, resting my head on the only thing I still had from our house. I have lived today, Papa. But Riva was gone.

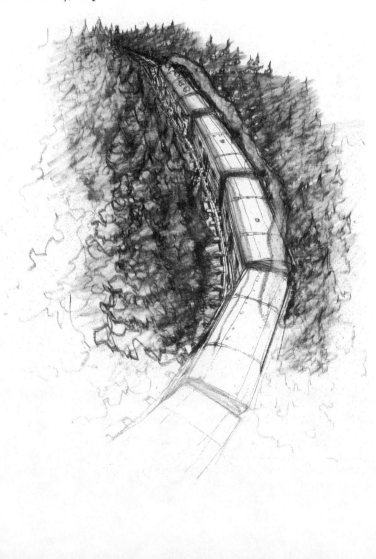

CHAPTER ELEVEN

Fall 1943

Before dawn Michal shook me awake and gave me more bread. "Stay on the path I will point out, and you will reach safety. The Nazis usually patrol where there are more people to terrorize. May God be with you."

I started walking, my steps awkward at first in the clogs. But after going barefoot, I was thankful for them. In a couple of hours I reached the village that was controlled by the partisans. I watched longingly as a peasant woman poured milk from a pitcher into a cup for her child. Where was my mother now? I looked around, knowing she wasn't there, yet seeing her face in every mother's face I saw.

But who would tell me how to reach Bielski's otriad? I could hear a blacksmith hammering metal. Down the street two men were loading sacks of potatoes into a wagon. Just then a younger man walked up to them. I couldn't see his face fully, but his dark hair and the way he moved his hands as he talked reminded me of Riva's brother Hersh. I watched, trying to get a better look. He turned after a couple of minutes and walked away from them. It was Hersh! What was he doing here? Did he know what happened to Riva? I ran up to him, telling him about the Nazis and the dogs.

"Riva escaped," he said. "She's with me and my family now."

"Where?" I looked around, expecting to see her.

"We're in hiding, on our way to Bielski's."

"Then I can go with you," I said, relieved. I wouldn't be alone from now on. I wouldn't have to find my own way.

But he started leaving. "We can't take on anybody else," he said impatiently, his back to me now.

How could he mean that? I began to follow him, pleading. "But if Riva and I hadn't been separated, we would both have found you."

He looked back at me coldly. "You'll have to find your own way." Then he walked on.

I stopped, feeling his words like a slap. Had Riva meant to leave me too? I felt people staring at me and began to walk through the village as if I knew where I wanted to go. A horse-drawn wagon was approaching with young men in it. Were they going to Bielski's? I started toward them, but a woman who was walking along the street caught my arm.

"No," she whispered. "Don't go with them. They are no good."

I looked at her, thinking she sounded like my mother.

"There will be other wagons coming through," she said, her eyes kind, "others who will take you into the forest to be with your people."

How did she know? "My brother is in the forest," I told her. But I shouldn't have said that. It was better not to talk too much, even about things I wished were true.

She sighed and turned to go into a house, leaving me outside alone.

I walked along the street slowly, looking at the simple wooden houses, wondering what they were like inside, looking at the small gardens near them, remembering the one we had had at the little caretaker's house. But mostly I watched for a wagon. Within an hour some men and women came along, guiding a small one without a horse. They spoke Yiddish, so I knew they were Jews.

I ran up to them. "Are you going to Bielski's?" I asked.

One of the men said they were.

"May I go with you?" This time I didn't expect that they would let me. I might have to wait for another group.

"Are you alone?" the man asked me.

"Yes." I would cry if I said anything more.

The man looked at the woman next to him. She nodded, then looked at the others. They all nodded in agreement.

"You must be prepared to walk for many kilometers," the first man said to me. "The Nalibocka Forest is huge. We may not reach the Bielski otriad for two days, and we aren't even sure exactly where the camp is. As for help from villagers along the way, they fear the Nazis as much as we do. Still, whatever we get to eat we'll divide among us all."

"I'm used to being hungry," I almost whispered.

His eyes softened. "I know." He gazed far away before looking back at me. "I'm Isaac, and this is my wife, Becky."

She smiled. "What is your name?"

"I'm Sarah, from Lida."

"Come," she said as they started walking again.

Relieved, I fell into step with them, not feeling quite so alone.

Before dark, we came to the remains of a burned village at the edge of the Nalibocka Forest. There was no sign of life, no smoldering fire.

"This happened days ago," Isaac said. "There is not even the smell of the disaster."

"A shed is still standing," one of the other men said.

Isaac walked toward it cautiously, and we followed.

"Wait!" He took out a gun. "I'll check first."

Let no one be there, I hoped as he pushed the shed door wide open.

"It's empty," he called, sounding relieved, and we all headed toward the shelter.

"Perhaps there are still potatoes in the fields," Becky said. And while some in the group searched for them, others built a fire. We found pieces of tin in houses that were not completely destroyed, and we made graters by punching holes in the tin with nails. Soon we were grating potatoes, making latkes as if it were Hanukkah.

The next morning we awoke to find that snow had fallen during the night. It looked magical now, clinging to branches and covering the fields.

"It's a miracle," someone said. "Snow in September!"

Or maybe a promise, I thought, that we would be safe soon and I would find David. But it was still hard for me to think of the world without Nazis. I shivered in the cold that had come overnight.

We walked into the forest, leaving footprints and wheel tracks behind us in the snow. They could lead the Nazis to us. But by midday the sun had melted the snow, and all that was left was water dripping from the branches, sounding like tiptoeing fairies from one of Chicava's tales.

Then we heard another sound, one that wasn't magical. Something or someone was moving near us. We stopped. Was it the Nazis? A wild animal? The trees and vines were bare. We must be easy to see, yet we could see nothing. My mother had said the forest could be more cruel than the ghetto, and my heart began beating so hard, I felt it all through my body. Isaac drew his gun from his belt.

Branches snapped as the sound got closer. Then between the trees we saw a man riding a horse slowly, but not uncertainly. They both seemed to know this wilderness. The man smiled and called out to us in Yiddish, quickly telling us he was from Bielski's otriad. "I'll take you the rest of the way." He kept riding toward us.

"He speaks Yiddish," people whispered to each other, wanting to believe he was a Jew.

Isaac held his gun without aiming it. "We know Bielski sends out guides," he said to his wife.

The man wore no uniform, but his boots looked like the ones the Nazis wore. His rifle was slung over his shoulder, yet he made no move to grab hold of it. I stared at his boots as he got closer.

He smiled at me when he noticed. "We got them when we ambushed some Nazi supply trucks," he told me.

I knew men from Bielski's otriad had done that, and I felt a little safer as he talked with Isaac.

"You have a weapon," the man said.

"One gun." Isaac still held it.

"Good! We need whatever weapons we can get. This is partisan territory now, but there are still roving bands of Nazis."

I wanted to ask if he knew David, but I was afraid. Could I trust this man who would lead us? Isaac seemed to, but I would wait before deciding.

Soon we were on our way, walking deeper and deeper into the Nalibocka Forest. There were no villages to pass now. There were no roads to follow anymore, and the wagon kept getting stuck as we followed the man on the horse through tangled vines and half-frozen swamps. How did he know which way to go?

Daylight began to disappear, first from the spaces between the trees, then from the sky. My legs moved stiffly, without feeling, as wooden as my clogs. David, David, are you still alive? Maybe I shouldn't have come after all.

But when I stumbled, Isaac's wife caught hold of my arm to keep me from falling. "Look ahead," she said finally. "We are almost there."

A clearing! I strained to make sense of what I saw in the dimness before dark. There were simple huts low to the ground on each side of something like a street. Partway down the street I could see taller tent-shaped buildings, their roofs covered with tree branches, smoke coming out of their chimneys. It was a little village in the wilderness. And there was no barbed wire.

The man on the horse turned around. "We are at Bielski's otriad." He chuckled. "Somehow we manage to live in spite of the Nazis. See the *ziemlankas?*" He pointed to the tent-shaped structures. "We are building more of them. They are mostly underground, except for their roofs. This winter we will have good shelter for everyone."

As we walked into the camp, I noticed men and women, as well as a few children, standing in a food line partway down the street. A huge kettle was hanging from a tree, a fire crackling under it. Those in the line looked at us but didn't step out of place. I searched their faces, looking for David's. He wasn't there. Where was he? My legs began to shake, and I fought to stand up.

Our guide dismounted as a tall, broad-shouldered man walked up to us.

"I am Tuvia Bielski," he said, his voice calm but strong.

We stood silent, exhausted, waiting for his words. But for the first time since leaving my parents, I began to feel safe.

"I don't promise you anything," he said. "We may be killed while we try to live. But we will do all we can to save more lives." Then he looked right at me, his eyes filling with tears. "What is your name, child?"

"Sarah," I answered. Then seeing his eyes searching, questioning, I told him, "I am from Lida." I pushed the weakness away. "My brother, David, may be here. I must find him." And without stopping, I told him how David and Lili had disappeared as the ghetto was being evacuated, and what had happened to my parents and Rachel.

He nodded, then put his finger to his lips to silence me. Turning to the man who had led us, he said, "See that they get soup." He put his hand on my shoulder. "Come."

As we walked silently down the street, past some small huts and large ziemlankas, I heard cows lowing and horses whinnying. Was that singing I heard? My steps began to feel light, as if I were wearing ballet slippers instead of wooden clogs.

Suddenly Tuvia Bielski stopped at one of the ziemlankas. He opened the door and led me down some stairs into a room below ground. It was lit by a stove in the center. Figures, dim in the shadowy light, turned toward us.

"Sarah!" The voice came from the darkness away from the stove. I ran toward him as he came into the light toward me. David lifted me up, holding me close. "You're here. You're alive," he said. Then I felt Lili's arms, too. At that moment there were no others, just the three of us living in this forest place till we could be free.

Sarah's Story

Escape to the Forest is based on the real experiences of a girl named Sarah who survived the German occupation of Lida and lived in Bielski's otriad with her brother and his wife beginning in September 1943. Her parents, along with the baby they cared for, were put to death in Treblinka, one of the Nazi extermination camps.

In July 1944, on orders from the Russian army, the otriad had to disband. Men of military age were sent to the front lines by the Russians to fight the Nazis. Sarah's brother worked for the railroad, so he was not sent into combat.

Before the Russians sealed their border, keeping all from leaving, Sarah, her brother and his wife were allowed to go to the western part of Poland. From there the Jewish underground helped them escape to Italy. Because they had family in the United States, they chose to wait in Italy till they would be allowed to emigrate to the United States. In 1948 they went to Philadelphia, at first living with an aunt, whose teenage daughter told Sarah to call herself Sheila. It was more American. In 1954, at the age of twenty-three, Sarah, now Sheila, married a man who was a survivor of a Nazi concentration camp. Sheila Garberman and her husband are the parents of two grown children, a son and daughter, both of whom are physicians.

More About Tuvia Bielski

Tuvia Bielski was born in 1906 in the little village of
Stankiewicze, located between the two larger towns of
Lida and Nowogródek, in what is now Belarus. He was one of
twelve children. While most Jews of that time lived in cities,
the Bielskis were peasants, earning their living as farmers. They
also owned a mill, but they were very poor.

The Bielskis were the only Jews in Stankiewicze, but they
observed Jewish traditions, walking to a nearby town each week
to go to religious services. From the beginning of the German
occupation Tuvia and two of his brothers, Asael and Zus, vowed
never to live in a ghetto. They lived hidden in the countryside
they knew, helped by gentiles. As the danger became greater,
they went into the forest.

The other partisans' main goal was to fight and defeat the
Germans, but Tuvia Bielski's primary mission was to save Jewish
lives. After the slaughter of most of the Jews in Lida in May
1942, he encouraged those left in the ghetto to escape and join
him and his family in the forest. By the fall of 1942 there were
about two hundred in his otriad, based in two connecting
forests. Always ready to move to avoid detection, they went
into the Nalibocka Forest in mid-1943. By now they numbered
seven hundred. Even though they were in a more remote area,

they were subjected to the "Big Hunt," a final assault by the Nazis, who entered the forest searching out partisan groups. Bielski led his people away from danger, and when the Nazis left, giving up their interest in controlling the forest, Bielski set to the task of building a more permanent community that included a doctor, nurses, tailors, barbers, carpenters and bakers. There was a little school for the children.

The Russians ordered the otriad evacuated in July 1944 and said that everything there had to be destroyed. They didn't want the Germans or any others to use the camp as a base for sabotage. Over twelve hundred Jews had been saved and walked from their forest refuge, protected by their armed fighters on either side of them. It had been the largest rescue of Jews by Jews during World War II.

Once out of the forest the Bielskis were looked upon with suspicion by the Russians as well. Asael was taken into the Russian army. He died in battle. Tuvia and Zus, along with their wives, escaped to Rumania. From there they went to what would become Israel. Both served in the Israeli army. Later they all emigrated to the United States, settling in New York City. Tuvia Bielski died at the age of eighty-one in 1987 and is buried in Israel.